LORDS OF RUIN

A REVERSE HAREM DARK COLLEGE BULLY
ROMANCE

RUTHLESS KINGS OF THORNHAVEN

SOPHIE J. RIVERS

PROLOGUE

D on't say you wouldn't do the same thing. If your father was drowning in debt from your hospital bills, I know you would also find yourself standing naked before three gloriously beautiful guys with a proposition and a check for one hundred thousand dollars.

Trust me, no one in my situation would turn that cash away, no matter how proud they are. But in this case, you're me, and your pride left you when you saw the foreclosure notice on your front door.

Your morals disappeared when you saw your giant teddy bear of a father crying as he held the only items you have left of your mother. You became fearlessly stupid when you heard him contemplate in hush whispers to your Aunt Nikki whether or not to sell your mother's engagement ring to cover a couple of nights in a motel.

When you're desperate to protect the only person in this world you love and have no other options, you'll do whatever it takes, *even if it means selling your soul to three guys who despise you more than anything, just like I did.*

1

WILLOW

"This is a stupid idea, Will," Jasmine mutters, fixing her mascara in the rearview mirror.

"Never said this was a smart idea; I just said it was an idea." I mess around with the faux septum ring in my nose.

Now that I'm eighteen, I want a real septum piercing, but Dad won't let me in case I get an infection. I have had this new heart in my chest for sixteen months, and most heart transplants are considered a success after four months, but my body can reject this heart at any time.

I will never truly be out of the woods. This heart saved me, but it will haunt me for the rest of my life.

"You want to steal from the King, Willow." Jasmine enunciates every syllable in my name, and I flinch, looking away from her and at my reflection.

My black hair with washed-out pink tips falls in loose curls around my shoulders, and my smokey eye makeup brings out the green in my hazel eyes. My skin has lost most of its vibrant complexion, and I am just getting some of my curves back after barely eating during my two years of hospitalization.

Jasmine's voice breaks me out of the trance I'm in. She cocks her head at me as if to emphasize how stupid of an idea it is. "We're going to get killed."

I roll my eyes. "No, we won't."

"Okay, so what's the plan, superstar? Are we just going to waltz up into the King of Thornhaven's place and enter like it's nothing when we weren't invited, and you're here to steal?"

I shrug, "He won't miss anything I take, and we look good. They aren't going to turn away two hot girls."

"Honey, there are like hundreds of hot girls walking up to the party right now."

I turn to look out the window at all the partygoers strutting up the driveway and into the 800 acres of the Beaumont estate for Vincent Beaumont's annual and last ABC party -- Anything But Clothes -- Birthday party.

There is a group of guys standing shirtless, displaying their toned and chiseled bodies. Some dressed in duct tape, plastic bags, and strategically placed cardboard pieces, while others have wrapped Saran Wrap around their torsos, leaving little to the imagination, or just some duct tape with a box covering their private areas, exposing the rest.

The girls, on the other hand, take it to the next level. Their outfits are works of art: newspaper dresses and bubble wrap that perfectly hug every curve. One girl confidently walks by in an ensemble made entirely of silk ribbons that barely hold together, leaving little to the imagination. Another boldly rocks a patchwork design of neon post-it notes, held together by body glue, revealing her long legs and smooth shoulders.

I am wearing four boxes of cereal cut up into a tube top stuck so close to my body the tape nips at me, a micro skirt that is so small my ass falls out of it, and my platform white leather boots.

I just hope the guard at the front, who is making sure everyone is following the strict anything but clothes rule, doesn't make me take off my underwear. Jasmine doesn't want to be here and sports a pair of black Converse and a black trash bag with three holes: one for her head and two for her arms. Her blonde mohawk has red highlights today.

"Look, I'll walk confidently, and you'll walk in with that glare you have permanently on your face, and boom! No one will turn us away, okay?" I nod at her before taking a deep breath and pushing the car's passenger side door open. My sparkly silver purse is swinging on my arm.

Jasmine quickly follows me, pulling on my elbow to whisper in my ear. "Did I forget to mention that Damien Sterling hates your fucking guts? Wait, in fact, all of the Chessmen hate you: The King. The Knight, even the fucking Rook. They all hate you."

"I thought best friends were supposed to be supportive?" I roll my eyes, pulling her forward towards the giant golden doors.

Jasmine isn't wrong; they all hate me.

Vincent Beaumont, also known as the King of Thornhaven, is the heir to this massive estate and finance genius in his own right. He has black hair that is always styled perfectly, piercing blue eyes that see into my soul, and a tailored school uniform that fits him like a glove.

Juan "Cast" Castillo, the Rook, is said to have ties to the cartel, but you wouldn't know he was crazy unless you saw him like I did. To everyone else, he is the silly class clown with messy, curly brown hair and a lazy smile that soaks panties and makes hearts do backflips. To me, he is a sadist who would love nothing more than to break me and happily lick the tears off my face.

But the one that really hates me and would love to see me fucking dead is the Knight, Damien Sterling. He isn't as rich as the other two; in fact, his mother worked as a maid for the Beaumonts and the Castillos, and he met Juan and Vincent while he tagged along with his mother as she worked for them over the weekends.

He shares a bond with the Chessmen through their mutual affection for Rosemary Sterling. Despite their reputation for not caring about anyone or anything, I know they loved Rosemary dearly. It was evident in their actions when she was diagnosed with cancer; they spared no expense and visited her every day.

When my myocarditis was so bad I couldn't leave the hospital, and everyone said I was a heart attack away from death, I would hang out with Rosemary in the hospital garden. She would give me her cherry jello and hug me tightly when no one else would in fear of breaking me. Her heart overflowed with kindness, making it almost overwhelming to be around her.

Damien's mother was perfect and the center of the Chessmen's worlds. So when he found out she died for me, that was it; he hated me. I was the reason he was now alone in the world.

I am the reason the only mother they ever had is dead, and they have all rights to hate me. I hate me. If I knew it was hers, I would have never taken it, but I didn't know until after the transplant was finished that Rosemary Sterling donated her heart to me. I didn't even know she was being tested to see if we were compatible.

Jasmine doesn't know any of this; she just thinks they're cruel, and I guess it is better to assume they are evil than to know how kind they can genuinely be. It only makes the looks they give me even more painful. It only makes me take my punishments at school like I deserve them because I do.

As we approach the sprawling 800-acre estate, I can't help but feel a mix of awe and anxiety wash over me. The Greek-inspired mansion looms before us, its towering white columns flashing different colors from the party lights, and intricate carvings decorate the sides.

The golden door at the entrance sparkles, invitingly like the gates of heaven—yet intimidating because I know nothing heavenly exists on the other side of that door.

A security guard, his muscular frame like a fortress, looms next to the golden doors, scanning the crowd of partygoers with hawkish intensity. He barely dodges a guy wrapped in a toga-like ensemble as he assesses the crowd. "Can't let you in, man," he declares, his voice cold and unyielding.

"What? Come on, man—these are not clothes; these are bed sheets!" the guy protests.

The guard shrugs dismissively. "Rules were changed: no bedsheets, curtains, or clothes-like fabric."

"Seriously?!" The guy's voice rises in disbelief, and I can sense the tension crackling in the air.

"Yeah, go change and come back," the guard retorts, a glint of satisfaction in his eye as he watches the guy's shoulders slump. With a groan, the rejected partygoer turns, stomping away, frustration radiating off him like heat waves.

I feel the weight of the guard's gaze shift to us as if he can smell the uncertainty wafting off our skin. Jasmine and I exchange a quick look, and I swallow hard.

A smarmy smile curls his lips, and I can feel my stomach churn with disgust. "Spin," he commands, and my heart races, a flash of anger igniting within me.

"What?" I snap, my eyebrows furrowing and fists balling up at my sides.

He leans in slightly, the smugness radiating off him like a foul odor. "No underwear allowed. It's part of the rules because it's technically clothes."

A pulse of heat surges through me, and I instinctively bristle, ready to tell him off. "Are you serious?" I demand. This guy must be a creep; there's no way he can be serious.

But then, he looks off to the side, and I follow his gaze to the clear bin beside him—overflowing with an array of colorful panties from other partygoers. "Sorry, sweetheart. I don't make the rules." He smiles, leveling his obsidian eyes with mine.

"Don't call me sweetheart." I roll my eyes, my heart thundering in my chest and my gut twisting in annoyance -- only the Chessmen would want every girl at this party commando. With a slight shimmy, I tug my cute white satin underwear with a dainty bow in the front, the sexiest underwear I own, down my thighs and over my boots.

I feel ridiculous and angry as I drop the delicate fabric into the bin with an exaggerated sigh, shooting the guard with a sarcastic look of compliance.

"There, happy?" I snarl, trying to mask the wave of vulnerability threatening to wash over me.

The guard's grin widens as he moves out of our way, "Enjoy, ladies."

"You didn't ask for my underwear," Jasmine narrows her eyes on him and places both hands on her hips.

The guard shoots both eyebrows up in confusion and looks around him as if she isn't talking to him. "Girl, I can tell by your face if anyone touches you, you will stab them."

Jasmine's grin sharpens, transforming her delicate features into something fierce and predatory. She laces her fingers through mine, squeezing tightly. "And you'd be absolutely correct!" She shoots back, her voice laced with playful menace. "Aren't you observant?"

Jasmine tugs me forward, and we step into the chaotic whirlwind of the party; the air is heavy with laughter, alcohol, and music. The moment we cross the threshold, I'm hit by a wave of noise and color, overwhelming my senses.

A group of our peers swirls around us, their bodies glistening under the vibrant lights, some already stumbling under the weight of drinks in their hands.

A couple nearby is locked in a passionate kiss, oblivious to the world, with their trash bags ripped open, exposing both girls' breasts, while naked acrobats twist through the air above, defying gravity in their silks.

"Welcome to the jungle," Jasmine whispers in my ear as she scans the room, rocking back on the heels of her feet.

My mind races as I assess the opulence surrounding us. Gold-plated fixtures shine like beacons, and clusters of expensive bottles are lining tables draped in silk. Art pieces worth thousands hang on the walls, and the laughter and chatter of Thornhaven's elite fill the air.

But I can't focus on the luxury right now; I need to think strategically. My eyes dart around the room, searching for the perfect item to steal—something that would fetch at least twenty grand, enough to keep our house from foreclosing. Just one thing, and I can figure out the rest later.

"Let's do a lap and see what I can grab," I whisper to Jasmine, suddenly distracted by the two girls grinding on each other.

"Just don't get caught," she warns, her voice low. "The Chessmen are going to be around here somewhere, and if they catch you..."

"I'll cross that bridge when I get there," I retort, trying to shake off the rising anxiety. I'm so close to saving my father and pulling us out of this mess. I just need to be smart about it.

Jasmine pulls me deeper into the crowd, and I can't help but marvel at the sheer absurdity of the party. A group of girls flits by in elaborate dresses made of bubble wrap, giggling as they bounce on their heels. The pulsating music seeps into my bones, blending with the energy of the people around me, and for a brief moment, I almost forget why I'm here.

"Look at that," Jasmine whispers, tilting her head to the right where an ornate silver vase is perched atop a marble pedestal near the entrance. It glimmers tantalizingly in the light, and I can already envision the price tag it must carry.

"That's a steal-worthy piece. But it's too exposed. Anyone could see us lift it." I huff, continuing to survey the room. I need to go upstairs to the jewelry, something small like a watch that I will probably have to hide between my butt cheeks, but it'll be worth it. Right when I am going to turn to Jasmine and tell her, that's when I see the first Chessman, Juan "Cast" Castillo.

Cast stands across the room, a figure carved from shadows and light, his emerald-green eyes glinting like polished gemstones. The flickering party lights catch the glitter dusted across his bare chest, making him shimmer like an earth bound god. He moves with an effortless grace, his body coiling and uncoiling like a serpent ready to strike, each motion smooth and deliberate as he dances.

His tousled and wild brown hair frames his chiseled features, drawing attention to his high cheekbones and the mischievous glint in his eyes. A playful smirk dances on his lips; one that looks inviting and sweet. He's dressed in a daring ensemble that barely conceals his toned physique—just a few strategically placed foil patches, duct tape, and an ornate belt hanging low on his hips.

The chaos of the party swirls around him--his presence demanding attention as if he's the sun and everyone else are mere planets caught in his orbit. I can feel myself drawn to him like prey to the colorful trance of their predator.

As soon as our gazes connect, everything else blurs out of focus. My heart races in my chest, and I can almost feel the electricity crackling between us. His intense stare bores into me, sparking a tingling sensation that runs through my body. He is no longer smiling, and my stomach drops, knowing that I am the reason he doesn't look so carefree anymore.

I pull my gaze away and whisper into Jasmine's ear. "I'll distract the crowd. You keep an eye out for the guards and the Chessmen. If anything goes sideways, bail."

Jasmine raises an eyebrow. "Don't get in trouble, Will, promise?"

"Trouble is just another word for opportunity," I smirk as I grab a shot off of a passing waiter's tray and down it, flashing her a huge grin. "Make sure Cast doesn't follow me."

2

VINCENT

She locks eyes with Cast, but I saw her first. Willow Cater, in my house, wearing four cereal boxes that barely cover her breasts and definitely don't cover her ass. I must thank Cast for his no-underwear rule; it'll make what I want to do to her so much easier.

I know we hate her, but there is a thin line between hate and lust, and fuck does she not teeter on the line of making me want to fuck her every day.

When we first met her, she had been sick for three years prior, and she looked hollow and broken, just like Rosemary looked the last time I saw her. She was a shell of a girl that I wanted to fill.

I wanted to make her our little slave for the rest of her life for taking away the only woman who has ever loved me, but Damien wouldn't have it.

Just looking at her made him sick, and since he was the one left alone in a broken-down apartment in the shitty part of town, he made the call on what we would do to Willow.

He decided we hated her, that we would make her wish she died instead of Rosemary, and while I think that's a waste of a perfect ass and hourglass figure, I wasn't the one who lost their biological mother.

I watch her from the balcony, shrouded in shadows, leaning forward on my throne with a joint hanging out of my mouth. I'm up here away from everyone because I'm not likable like Juan, or in love with the limelight like Damien.

I hate parties.

I only have this fucking party to reestablish what everyone knows: I am King of Thronhaven, and I keep my subject satiated. At every party I make a grand entrance, pick the girl I want in my bed tonight, fuck her and then go to sleep.

Willow whispers to her friend and then snakes her perfect ass through the crowd, looking cautiously over her shoulder when she reaches the grand staircase leading up to the private rooms upstairs. She slides past the velvet rope with a distinct 'Do Not Enter' sign hanging on it.

A low chuckle rumbles through my chest—*naughty girl* sneaking into forbidden areas. She will need to be punished, and I know the perfect way to do so.

I stamp the joint out on the railing and move through the dark hallways to the other side of the house, which is too fucking big for me, my stepmother, Angie, and her two children, both under the age of ten, both in boarding school.

My father and Angie are on their annual February trip to England on my birthday, and unless you count the silent servants, I live here alone most of the time.

I have twenty-five bedrooms, fifteen bathrooms, six half-bath-rooms, three pools, a music room with a professional-grade recording studio, a tennis and basketball court, a mini-museum, Rosemary's untouched art studio, a library, and, of course, a greenhouse all to myself.

I would like it if Damien also lived here, but he refuses to leave the apartment he lived in with his mother. Juan and I take turns paying the rent, and sometimes we stay there, too, because it feels more like home than either of our houses.

I keep walking until I see a tiny sliver of light flooding the hallway, and my lips quirk because the little devil found my room out of all the rooms in this house. *How lucky am I?*

I lightly push the door open, and she doesn't notice. Her body is hunched over the glass case in the corner, filled with watches, cufflinks, diamond earrings, and a platinum, diamond-encrusted, Jesus-piece chain Cast got me as a joke. I may be old money, but Cast's money goes longer than mine, and while he claims he's just a billionaire, I swear he's a trillionaire.

Willow's hands run along the edges of the case; she shakes it once, trying to lift the top. Her cereal skirt rides up with the movement, and I can see her round ass peeking beneath the *Foot Loops* mascot. *Fuck* she looks so goddam delectable; her tiny waist is on display, and I can see she has fucking back dimples.

My cock swells against my makeshift bubble wrap shorts as I imagine how perfect those divots are for my thumbs to fit into when I rail her from the back.

If it weren't for that thought, she wouldn't have heard the bubble wrap pop.

3

WILLOW

Vincent Beaumont is staring at me. His eyes are so low like he is struggling to keep them open, but the smile on his lips is sharp and predatory, and I almost want to run out the double doors to the left of me and see what would happen if I jumped off the balcony.

"Well, this is a nice surprise." He drawls, his voice smooth and low, laced with an undertone that sends heat between my legs, and I am very aware of how little 'clothes' I have on right now.

"You would think it was my birthday, little Willow Cater in my room barely dressed, the perfect present." The words roll off his tongue like honey, sweet yet tinged with something darker, something sexier. He stalks deeper into the room, his tongue runs across his bottom lip, as his eyes flicker down.

"I'm not a present for you." I rush the words out of my mouth, and my eyes dart around the room, looking for an escape that won't result in broken limbs.

Vincent pouts, with faux sadness on his face. "Then you came in here to surprise me? How sweet are you?"

"No," I cough out before I can really think about it, but even if I did I can't distract Vincent with sex. I'm a virgin and I can't give my virginity to Vincent Beaumont, especially if his dick is popping bubble wrap. It might kill me.

When he is only a step away from me he leans forward, hovering over me. "Then why are you here?"

His ice-like eyes look like they're melting in the dim lighting, and I almost take a step forward to see them more clearly. "I-I was looking for something." I stutter. *That's fucking great Will just keep talking.*

"Looking for what?" He growls, and his eyes open wider, so I look away from him because something about Vincent's gaze makes me feel like he could take my soul away, but when my eyes flicker over his shoulder I meet with the stormy gray eyes of Damien.

My mouth is agape, and now my throat feels dry, and my eyes are shifting across the room desperately. Vincent looks over his shoulder at Damien who is still standing in the hallway staring at me, arms crossed with metal chains in layers over his chest and groin. His blonde buzzcut has an intricate, swirling black design on the right side and he looks like a demon ready to drag me to his lair. My thighs shift as I feel tingles running across my skin, and a buzzing around my center.

Vincent clicks his tongue at me, pinching my chin and dragging my gaze back to his. "Look at me little devil, why are you here in my room, touching my jewelry case practically naked?"

I lick my lips, and Vicent's eyes drift down to them, a growl rising in his chest. "Don't tease me when I have to punish you."

My eyes widen. "P-punish me?"

"Mmmhmm." Cast's playful tone drifts into the room, as he slides past Damien and makes his way inside. His tan skin glistening in sweat, and eyes blown wide, with excitement brimming around the edges. "Your friend already spilled."

Cast jumps onto the king size bed, covered in a gray comforter with black sheets peeking out.

I scoff, pulling my head away from Vincent's pinching grip. "No way, Jasmine would never."

"She would if I threatened to rip that pitiful trash bag and make her walk out of here naked." Cast shrugs, leaning back on his arms, and running his tongue along the inside of his mouth.

"She's not afraid of showing off her body." I snap, narrowing my eyes on Casts smug face. "She's the girl who skinny dipped at Asher's party last month."

"Really?" Vincent smiles, leaning away from my personal space. He taps a finger against his chin, and turns towards the door. "She has a killer body. Maybe I should go get her, make her talk."

My stomach twists sharply, a bitter taste rising in my throat as the word escapes before I can reel it back in. "No!"

"No? Then tell me little devil why are you in here." Vincent levels his eyes with mine, and I notice Damien is leaning against the archway, closer in the room.

I don't open my mouth, and instead look down at the platform leather white boots I am wearing, rubbing the sole into the ground.

"She's trying to steal boys." Cast laughs, and my eyes shoot up to look into his crazed expression like a cat who just caught a mouse between their teeth. "Oh, did I mention I threatened to slice up that body of hers with a knife? She was going to leave here naked and bloody."

I feel sick. Jasmine is probably scared out of her mind and long gone now. I would be too. I can't blame her.

Damien snorts as he steps forward, closing the door behind him with a soft click. He leans back in a chair across from me, his expression cold, detached. "Not surprising she's a thief," he mutters, the first words he's bothered to say tonight, each one laced with disdain.

A surge of rage catches me off guard, burning through the humiliation tightening in my chest. My nostrils flare as I meet his stare head-on. "I need the money," I spit out, my voice raw and trembling with anger.

The room falls silent for a beat, the tension thick enough to suffocate me. Cast's wild eyes dance with a dangerous kind of excitement, and Vincent's gaze sharpens like a blade. He stands a little too still, that predator smile tugging at his lips, so dark and unreadable.

"And what are we supposed to do about that, hmm?" Vincent finally speaks, his voice low, dangerous. He takes a step forward, his smile never wavering. "Stealing from us isn't exactly the smartest way to solve your little problem, is it?"

Cast tilts his head, like a cat toying with an injured bird. "You know what happens to thieves, don't you? I'm dying to see what we should do with you."

I swallow hard, my heart pounding in my chest. "I didn't have a choice," I murmur, my voice cracking under the weight of desperation. "We're going to lose the house. My dad is drowning my medical bills."

Vincent's faux pout returns, and leans in closer than he did before. "And what are we supposed to do about that, little devil?"

"Be decent and help me." My eyes dart to each of the guys' eyes, but they offer no sympathy. "You and Cast have so much money you can spare a few thousand."

Damien snorts again, but I ignore it. Cast jumps up on the bed, with a mad look on his face. "A few thousand?!"

"I need at least twenty thousand." I whisper. "Just to keep our head above water, if not we have to sell the house and I need to move to Minnesota with my Aunt and her four kids."

Vincent clicks his tongue again, curling one of my pink strands behind my ears. "No, no, no. You can't leave me."

"How much do you need to keep your house and pay off your medical bills?" Cast asks, leaning forward on his knees.

I keep my eyes on Vincent as I answer. "One hundred-fifty thousand dollars."

Cast whistles slowly at the amount, but Vincent smiles like a Cheshire cat. "Excuse us for a moment, little devil."

4

CAST

Vincent pulls Damien and me into the dark hallway, which flashes blues and purples from the party lights downstairs. The music is a dull, muffled sound that shakes the floor underneath my sandals. Vincent is smiling like he just caught some new prey, Damien looks annoyed, and I feel a surge of adrenaline running through my body.

Willow Cater is damn near naked in Vincent's room; why *the hell am I not already balls-deep in my Chiquita right now?* I can make her say sorry with my handprint on her ass and my mouth wrapped around her perfect chocolate nipples that are peeking from beneath her cereal top. Fuck how am I ever going to eat Frosted Flakes without a hard-on now?

My cock is hardening against the foil, and the pricks of the material only make me harder. I love pain: receiving, giving. I can't cum without it, and it's been that way my whole life. The same way I've wanted to ruin Willow since she came back to school Junior year, healthy, sexy as all hell, in her punk outfits, and hair that constantly changes colors. Right now the roots and undercut are pink and I like it.

Vincent closes the door with a click and whirls to Damien with wild eyes, but before he can say anything Damien speaks first. "No."

"No?" I snap, rage rising in my chest.

"You're not fucking the girl who killed my mother, our mother." Damien eyes land with mine, but I look away and roll my jaw.

Vincent huffs, running his hand across his face and turning his back to us. Vicent has wanted to be with Willow since he first saw her on the first day of freshman year, but then a month later she was sick, and being homeschooled. Two years later she took Rosemary's heart and then Damien put a ban on her.

Vincent shakes his head, poking Damien in the chest. "This is not your call."

"What the fuck do you mean this is not my call? She has *my* mother's heart in her?" Damien growls in Vincent's face.

Vincent scoffs, looking off to the side. "I thought she was *our* mother a minute ago."

I step in between Vincent and Damien, placing a hand on both of their chests, and relishing in the fact that I am taller than both of them. "Tranquilos, chicos. She's just a girl, let's talk. D made the call when it came to *our* mom, but she just tried to steal from Vincent, a totally different situation."

It's funny how I have the most violent upbringing, and the more violent tendencies but when it comes to Vincent and Damien I find the nerve to be the peacekeeper.

"No, I said fucking no." Damien snarls squaring up to me, but I chuckle and pat his chest.

"Okay, but if she doesn't get this money she is moving to Minnesota. I don't know about you but I'm not traveling a thousand miles from Texas to Minnesota to torture her."

Damien rolls his jaw. If there is anything I know about Damien when it comes to Willow it's that she can't leave him, not when she has the only living part of his biological mother beating within her chest, so there's our bargaining chip.

I want to corrupt her, Vincent wants to consume her and Damien just wants her near to torture her and himself. He feels like he should have known his mother was sick. Colon cancer takes years to develop, as bad as hers had become, and he feels like he should have known that she was ill, despite him being a child at the time.

"She needs one hundred-fifty thousand dollars." Damien mumbles.

"Okay, and?" I question, shrugging my shoulders and stepping back from the two, now that the tension has eased. "I wipe my ass with that amount every morning."

"That's nothing to you, but valuable to her. She's going to need to pay us back." Vincent muses, a cold smile spreading across his lips, and when heat flashes across his gaze I smile too.

"I know a couple of ways..." I drawl, nodding my head as Vincent and I come to the same conclusion. Vincent and I might as well be twins because we're always thinking the same thing.

"She can be our servant, completely devoted to us, until the end of senior year." Vincent nods, looking over at Damien who stares into the darkness with a vacant look in his eyes.

"I just want her here." Damien mutters. "I don't care what you do with her."

Vincent clasps one hand on my shoulder, and the other on the back of my neck bringing me forward to rest his forehead against mine with a devilish gleam in his eye. "Cast, buddy, flip a coin. Pussy or throat?"

5

WILLOW

"Wait, you're giving me one hundred-fifty thousand dollars?" I gasp, the check dangles in front of my eyes, pinched between Cast's thumb and pointer.

Vincent's chin rests on my right shoulder, his cheek pressed against mine, and I can feel the smile on his face. "Just for you little devil."

My fingers twitch with the urge to rip it out of Cast's hands and flee, throwing caution to the wind. I can already feel my heart pounding in my chest at the mere thought of running to save my father from foreclosure. But I know these guys too well.

I glance at Damien, who has made it his life's mission to make my existence a living hell. His piercing gaze sends shivers down my spine, a constant reminder of his power over me.

No one ever talks to me without fear or disdain in their eyes. I am constantly bullied and ostracized by everyone around me. My short hair is a result of his girlfriend putting gum in it, and I've been banned from all parties because of him.

The saddest part? No boy has ever asked me out because I am deemed untouchable by the entire town.

The Chessmen have always hated me, but right now they offer me my salvation. I know it can't be out of kindness or pity because they would need a heart for that and I know none of the Chessmen have a heart.

"What's the catch?" I whisper.

Vincent's lips graze against my neck as he speaks. "You have to pay it back."

"With interest!" Cast adds.

My breath catches in my throat, how the hell, when the hell would I ever have the money to pay them back. It may take my entire life, but can I pass up this opportunity? No, when will I ever have this much access to this much money again? How else will I save my father from financial ruin?

My eyes flicker to Cast. "How long will I have to pay you back?"

Vincent's laughter rumbles along my skin and I feel like I can't fucking breathe. Cast's eyes twinkle with need and he shakes his head 'no' at me.

"We don't want your money Chiquita. We want you." Cast smiles.

"Me?" I gasp, and I can't help it. My eyes lock with Damien's across the room. His face is blank besides the fire glistening in his eyes.

Vincent's lips graze against my shoulder, and Cast pinches my chin drawing my eyes back to his. "You'll be our little pawn. To use, abuse...fuck."

Fuck? Fuck. My body shakes, and I feel myself paling under Cast gaze. I can't give them this part of me. They've taken everything good about living away from me. I can't also give the Chessmen my virginity. Vincent's laughter rolls across my skin again, as his lips suck on my pulse.

"Her heart is beating so fast." Vincent mumbles.

Cast's thumb slides across my bottom lip, a faux pout on his face. "You want to fuck us Chiquita?"

"N-no." My voice is more breathy than I intend, and Cast painfully grips my chin, pulling me closer to him.

"No?" Cast growls.

"I'm a virgin." I whisper, my eyes drifting down as my cheeks heat.

"Virgin?" Vincent clicks his tongue. "I don't believe you."

"I am." I choke out, my voice trembling as tears are welling up in my eyes.

My heart races with fear and anger, their leering grins reminding me of all the torment they've put me through. They want to take away my virginity, my first kiss, and they want me to be their pawn. But they can't take away the things I'm saving for someone who truly loves me. Is it worth risking homelessness for someone who genuinely wants me? My father and I may end up on the streets if I do not comply with their demands. I dry swallow, trying to slow down my heart and catch my breath.

"You hear that Damien? She's a virgin." Cast sings.

"Do you believe her?" Damien grumbles.

Cast catches my eyes again, looking for something, before he nods slightly. "I believe her."

"P-please," I stammer, my hands pinching the circle boxes around my hips. "I beg of you, please... I want to keep... I want to keep my virginity."

"Aww," Cast pouts, as Vincent's hands snake around my waist, resting on my stomach. "Beg louder baby, I like it."

I inhale sharply, my brows furrowing and spine bone straight. My gaze drifts to Damien, because he hates me so much that he would never want me, especially in a sexual way. Maybe my naked body would disgust him and he would not want me to suffer, but Damien's expression darkens as he steps forward, his gaze cold and unwavering.

"She said she wants to keep her innocence intact," he states firmly. "You will respect her wishes."

Vincent and Cast exchange a glance before breaking into mocking laughter. "Oh, how noble of you, Damien," Vincent sneers, taking a step back. "You'll stay intact for now little devil, but you still need to be punished."

I feel a chill run down my spine as their words hang heavy in the air. Damien leans back in his chair, a locked jaw and intense stare on me.

I breathe a sigh of relief, but my heart is still racing from the encounter. Vincent rests his head against my back. His warm breath against my neck makes my skin tingle, but I refuse to give him the satisfaction of knowing I'm still affected by his closeness.

Vincent's voice is deep and commanding. He smells like rain and smoke as he skims his nose up the column of my neck. "I want you to undress for us. Slowly. Let me see every inch of you."

I swallow hard, my mouth dry as I obey, knowing this is my only shot of saving myself and my father. My hands shake slightly as I reach for the edges of the cereal boxes, pulling at the tape holding it against my breast.

"Look at me Chiquita." Cast growls and my eyes lock on his as I rip the tape off my skin, my nerves too high to feel the sting of the tape ripping off of my chest and let the boxes fall to the floor.

Cast's eyes darken, and my skin feels like a thousand sparks of electricity run across my skin.

"Good girl," Vincent murmurs, stepping closer. His fingers brushing against the side of my breast, my nipples harden painfully at his touch, but I don't dare make a noise and I keep my eyes locked on Cast.

"Bottoms next." Cast challenges and I suck my dry lip back into my mouth.

His words send a thrill down my spine and I betray myself whimpering softly. The heat between my legs builds, and I press them closer together. Vincent's fingertips brush along the edge of the cereal box on my right hip, his voice rolls into my ear like thick molasses.

"You heard him, little devil. Bottoms off." Vincent encourages me.

I refuse to let my mind wander, knowing that if I do, I will run away and never return. But then I see Damien, his dark eyes fixed on me as he leans forward with his elbows planted firmly on his knees. Without hesitation, I grab the cardboard between my fingers and tear it apart, dropping the box to the ground without a second thought.

"¡Dios mío!" Cast mutters under his breath, and my eyes shoot back to Cast's face as his eyes trace the curve of my silhouette.His intense gaze roams over my exposed skin, and I can feel all three sets of their eyes lingering on every curve, every freckle, every scar on my body.

"It's even better than I've imagined." Vincent praises, his hands leaving a cold gust around my waist. "Spin for us."

I can feel the heat rising to my cheeks as I try to maintain my composure, masking the discomfort that bubbles beneath the surface. With a forced smile, I oblige, twirling slowly in front of them, feeling their stares like a physical touch upon my skin.

Vincent watches with a hunger in his eyes, a smirk playing on his lips and arms crossed casually over his chest.

The room feels suffocating, the air thick with tension and unspoken desires. As I turn back to face Cast, he steps forward, his hand reaching out to brush a lock of hair behind my ear. His touch ignites a fire within me that I try desperately to suppress. "On your knees, Pawn."

My chest tightens and I almost ask where the nickname Chaquita went and why he is now calling me Pawn, but instead I sink to my knees, eyes locked on his. Vincent follows me down, spreading his knees so my ass is pressed against the tented bubble wrap.

He cups my breasts in his hands, his thumbs teasing the sensitive skin around my nipples. I gasp, arching into his touch. "Feel how much I want you, Willow," he whispers, his breath hot against my ear. "Every part of you is mine. I won't ever let you go now."

My lips part, a small gasp leaving my lips, and Cast gives me a knowing smile. "She's so eager," he says, low and approving as his thumb slides across my bottom lip.

Vincent smiles against my jaw, his finger lightly pinching my nipples into little tents. "Now, I want you to touch yourself. Show me how wet you are for me."

My cheeks flush with embarrassment, as I bite my lip and look away. There is no way he knows how tight the coil of desire is in my belly. How would he know how his touch makes my brain foggy and all I want is to release whatever tension that's building in me. I have never touched myself, never had a reason to, but having their eyes on me makes my thighs slick with want.

I lift my hand to my chest, squeezing my breast gently the same way Vincent did when I first dropped my top. I pinch my nipple between my fingers, rolling it until I gasp. Cast's thumb slides deeper into my mouth, he tastes crisps like grapes and I have to force myself to keep my mouth open to suck on his thumb.

Vincent's hand wraps around mine guiding it lower. "No, not like that," he instructs. "Use your other hand. Touch your pussy. Make yourself moan for me."

My breath hitches as I move my hand from my breast to my pussy, feeling the slick heat already pooling there. Vincent chuckles again as my hand stays hovering over my pussy, not knowing where to touch, or what to do, but thanking the heavens that Jasmine insists on getting waxes together even if she is the only one sexually active until now.

"Slide your fingers into your wetness." He moans. "I know your fucking soaked for us."

He's not wrong; the minute I slide my fingers between my pussy lips I feel practically an ocean between them, and I close my eyes, involuntarily moaning as I explore.

"From the way she looks, I don't think she really wants to be a pure little virgin. She wants to be our little slut." Cast taunts me, and despite me knowing I should bite his thumb for calling me a slut, desire rolls through my stomach and I want him to say it again.

Damien growls at his words and my eyes open to see him white-knuckle gripping his knees across the room. Cast chuckles. "Eyes on me, Pawn. He can join at any time he wants, and don't worry—Vinny and I will keep our word—no deflowering."

"No deflowering tonight," Vincent moans. "But don't worry, I am going to be the one to pop that little cherry of yours. Now run your finger up to where you are pulsing with need."

I run my two fingers up to the bundle of nerves, and my body jolts, forcing Cast's thumb deeper into my mouth.

"She found her clit boys." Vincent mocks me and I flick my tongue out along Cast's thumb, needing to do something with my mouth.

He moans lightly, cursing under his breath. "Mierda!'

I know that word. It means shit, and from the way his green eyes look almost like the dark green of a forest after a rainstorm, I know I am doing something right. I flick it again and his lips curl into a dangerous smile as he pushes his thumb deeper down my throat. I cough, and then moan as the nerves around my center flutter like butterfly wings.

"You like that, Pawn?" Vincent groans in my ear, pushing his growing cock into the curve of my ass. "You like when Cast forces you to take it?"

I moan, nodding my head yes as my body is on fire. The pleasure too intense. I rub slow circles around the nerves that Vincent called my clit, whatever that is. and push harder on it making me jerk my body against my fingers as I chase the high, the sparks across my flesh, the building need growing in my belly.

Casts grabs a fistful of my hair, massaging the scalp with bruising force as he exchanges his thumb for two fingers and plunges them down my throat. "Suck it," Cast commands, and like a good Pawn I obey.

The force of his fingers and the prickle of pain from his grip in my hair makes me groan, the pain mingling with pleasure, making me even wetter. I rock against my hands, as Vincent cups my left breast with one hand and draws lines up my inner right thigh with the other.

"That's it," Vincent groans, his hand leaving my breast and gripping my hip, pushing me to grind on my fingers harder and take Casts fingers deeper. "Take it, and make yourself cum."

I shudder, my legs shaking with need as the pressure grows. I suck Casts fingers like a popsicle on a hot day. "Fuck, you're good at that," he mutters. His eyes shining so bright I feel almost honored to be on my knees for him. "You're missing out Damien. Our girl is a perfect little slut."

Fuck, there goes that word again. My body shutters slightly a little and my clit is throbbing to the point where I don't think I should touch it anymore. I go to move my hand away and Vincent grips my wrist.

"Don't you dare stop touching my clit. Keep fucking going." He growls and every hair on my body stands at attention as I pout, moving my fingers back to the nerves and torturing myself with slow circles. "Faster, little devil."

I speed up, my fingers still working my clit furiously. One of Vincent's hands leaves me and I hear a cacophony of bubble wrap popping before feeling something warm and fleshy is pressing against my entrance. My eyes shoot open and I lock my eyes with Cast.

Damien's voice growls from across the room. "Vincent."

Vincent positions himself so that the hard member sits right below my clit and my finger brushes against it with every circle I make around my clit. "Don't worry, I'm just showing Pawn something."

He grinds against me, and my body feels like it is seconds from burning to ash. I suck on Cast's finger harder. The combination of my sensitivity, the taste of Cast's fingers, Vincent's cock rubbing against me and Damien's eyes makes me feel out of breath, like I am at the top of a roller coaster about to tip over.

Vincent continues to grind against me. His fingers are pinching my nipples hard enough to make me cry. "Feel how much I want to claim you," he whispers. "How badly I want to fuck those tight walls."

Jeez. Vincent talks so freaking dirty. My vision blurs with tears and the pressure is building in my core; the tension reaches a fever pitch. I open my eyes, Cast's head is thrown back, his grip so tight on my head I know there will be strands of pink and black in his fists. Vincent's groans in my ear make me grind on him faster, but when my eyes lock with Damien a crescendo happens.

His dark, hungry eyes are locked on my body and in that moment, everything clicks into place. I fall over the cliff, the energy rushing through me feels like euphoria, like something clicked and now every ounce of tension has disappeared. My heart beats harder than it ever has in my chest and I feel like it's going to pop. Vincent groans in my ear, followed by stickiness coating my inner thighs. I think he reached that pitch too.

"Shit." Cast groans, pulling his fingers out of my mouth. "You made me cum in my fucking pants."

My eyes widen and I think Cast is going to punish me for causing him to cum in his tin foil pants, but instead he leans down in my face, pinching my chin with his wet fingers. "Next time I will make you clean it up."

I dry swallow, and Vincent laughs like this is the best day of his life. I look up, and relax into his warm embrace, then I hear Vincent's door slam shut, and then both Vincent and Cast break into laughter.

"W-what's funny?" I whisper, looking between the two, my body feeling like there is a continuous crackling across my skin.

Vincent's lips press against my shoulder, as Cast walks away towards a side door, where I assume the bathroom is.

"Don't worry little devil. Just know, you're ours now."

Thank you for reading the introduction to The Lords of Ruin, I hope you enjoyed it. Please leave me a review to help me grow, and share it with your fellow readers.

As a new independent author, your support means everything to me. Follow me on Amazon to be the first to know when the next book becomes available on Pre-order and when I have amazing deals.

Book One: Lords of Ruin:OWNED Is LIVE ...continue reading it now Free in Kindle Unlimited and available on paperback.

More from my desk.

Warm up for the holidays with Josie and her NFL hockey star whose only game is earning her with every puck.

Here is a taste of their angsty and steamy ride to a Merry Christmas with Triplets.

Pucking Christmas Triplets Surprise: A Surprise Pregnancy Dark College Hockey Romance

Christopher

Don't tell ESPN, but Josie Richards is the real reason I left the Mississippi Titans after an award-winning season: to come to this small town in Maine to coach a subpar hockey team. I did this not because I was humble or knew my prime was over, which isn't true. I am a beast driven by my obsession. If I wanted to be in my prime, I could be so for as long as I wanted.

No, it was for Josie Richards, Northbrook University darling with a smart mouth, killer legs and no fucking respect.

I remember watching her when I was at the top of my game last season. She looked like an angel, lost in the flurry of snow. She was Olympic-bound, a future gold medalist, and the icon everyone had their eye on. I mean, how could you not keep your eyes on her?

Her loose, wavy blonde hair with honey highlights looked effortlessly perfect even when tossed into a messy bun on her head. Up close, her tan freckles dusted her nose and cheeks, and her lips were a dusted baby pink. But the best part about being this close to her are those ivy-green eyes that remind me of the trees around my home in Michigan.

She is stunning, but she's still a student, even if she's a senior in college. This doesn't make my attraction to her any less inappropriate or complicated, but she is the reason I took this job below my status.

See, my obsession with the game consumed me daily: the sound of skates scraping against the ice, the roar of the fans, and the grunts of my opponents. But nothing compared to the adrenaline rush I felt when I stepped onto the ice for a game. Or so I thought until I saw her in her proper form.

Suddenly, the ice and the game didn't hold the same appeal for me anymore. Hockey felt dull, my contract was up, and Josie was ripe for the taking. It didn't matter that I spent my life dedicated to hockey when there was someone more compelling than hockey ever was.

The moment I laid eyes on Josie Richards, she caught me in her spell. It was during the Northbrook Winter Showcase, where I had been sent for good publicity after my team caused a drunken brawl at a local bar with some students from Northbrook.

I attended to show that not all of the Mississippi Titans are assholes, especially not their very own golden boy Christopher Jackson— killer on the ice, sweetheart in the city. I was to smile, wave, take pictures, and congratulate the performers.

I never would have guessed that a girl with blonde hair, wearing a sparkling lavender bodysuit and tutu, could capture my attention for the entire evening. The light from the stadium made her outfit look like a second layer of sparkling skin, hiding not a single curve from my imagination. Her toned legs curved in arches for tricks, making me wonder how many positions I could put her in.

But it wasn't just her physical prowess that held me captive. There was a fire in her eyes, a determination that burned brighter than the spotlight that followed her every move. She was a goddess, and the ice was her altar. I've never been big on prayer, but I've always believed in devotion and worship. Josie Richards' tight little body deserved to be worshiped in the most primal and passionate of ways, as a true believer would offer themselves to their goddess.

She was flawless on the ice—graceful, precise, and only making one minor mistake on a spin that no one noticed but me. She seemed perfect, living up to being the Olympic-bound gold medal star everyone had hyped her up to be. If it weren't for the tightness in her jaw, I'd think she was perfect, just like everyone else, but that's the thing about goddesses—they're just as human as us.

Off the ice at the afterparty in the president's house, she was polite, respectable, and stiff, giving everyone a plastered-on smile as she rolled her jaw over and over again. She had changed into a short, body-con, champagne dress that blended so well with her complexion that I had to remind myself over and over again that she had clothes on. When she was mine, and trust me, she would be, I would never allow her to wear that color again.

I watched from across the room at her performance, not knowing if this one or the one on the ice was better.

Every Tom, Dick, and Harry congratulated her, took a picture with her, and touched her. That's what really pissed me off; the number of men that found a reason to touch her, whether it was a hand on the small of her back during a photo, pinching her elbow to get her attention, moving a rogue curl behind her ear while they chatted; every man had tried to steal a piece of my little ice princess.

Lucky for their limbs, she was too cold to let any of that get to her. She excused herself halfway through the night, making an excuse about homework, and steadily exited the house.

After taking one last sip of my drink and flashing a few more polite smiles, I signed an autograph for the son of someone from Human Resources. But let's be honest: from the way she gripped my arm and licked her lips, little Johnny probably doesn't even exist. I winked in her direction and excused myself to the bathroom, but as soon as I saw my ice princess leave, I snuck out of the presidential house and followed her discreetly to wherever she was going.

I had seen the irritation in her face all night long. She absent-mindedly twirled a lock of her golden hair around her finger that she tugged from her bun, the same curl men kept tucking behind her ear. She was too annoyed to notice the romantic gesture. When she felt no eyes on her, she would furrow her brows and chew on the corner of her pinked glossed lips, frankly driving me mad all night. It only made me want to pull her lip between my teeth and bite it properly, kiss her properly.

The crisp air nipped at my cheeks as I entered the ice rink. I could see her slender figure already lacing up her skates, hidden beneath the bleachers. She seemed to be muttering to herself with a sense of urgency.

Gone was the image of the ice princess I had once been fascinated with. Instead, I watched as she angrily yanked her hair out of its perfect bun and marched onto the glistening ice. The blades of her skates cut through the smooth surface, leaving behind deep grooves in their wake. Her movements were powerful and determined, like a warrior preparing for battle on a frozen battlefield.

She glided across the ice with fierce grace, like a predator honing in on its prey. My little hellion drilled her blades into the ice, carving a path with precision and determination. She repeated the same combination relentlessly, her eyes blazing with the intensity of an obsessive athlete on a mission to perfect her craft.

As I watched from the shadows, hidden behind the bleachers, I couldn't tear my eyes away from her. Josie wasn't performing for an audience now and wasn't giving the polite, rehearsed routine that had the crowd eating out of her hand at the showcase. This was raw, unfiltered. She wasn't skating to dazzle; she was skating to destroy.

Her anger made her movements sharper and more aggressive. She dug her blades into the ice with purpose, spinning and leaping in a furious ballet that looked more like an attack than an art form.

Before, I had been intrigued. I wanted to see if the ice princess cracked, but now with this fire blazing off of her, *fuck,* I wanted to feed off of her; if this is the real her, I want all of it.

That guttural howl that only leaves the throat of an athlete that has beaten themselves over the head and came out covered in the blood of their desire to succeed.

The girl everyone saw at the parties, smiling and perfect in her champagne dress, wasn't the real her. No, this was. The tension in her jaw, the way she slammed down after each jump, the rage radiating from her every movement—that was the Josie Richards I was drawn to. Not the ice princess, but the warrior who fought her battles on the frozen stage. My little hellion.

I stepped closer, the sound of her skates cutting through the ice echoing in the empty rink. She didn't know I was there and didn't need to. I liked that this moment was mine. She was skating for me, and I soaked up every moment, from her face, flushed from exertion, to her loose hair stuck to the sweat on her neck, to the snarl permanently on her face.

She practiced until she screamed. Every time she faltered, she growled in frustration. That guttural howl that only leaves the throat of an athlete who has beaten themselves over the head and came out covered in the blood of their desire to succeed.

And god, I thought I had wanted her before when she was a little princess, but nothing compared to her now. She had a burning fire inside her that matched my obsession, my own relentless need to win. And I have won hundreds of games on the ice, rarely losing one— but her and her fierce, raw, unrelenting passion? I wanted every part of it. I fucking needed it like I needed air to breathe.

But don't worry, she'll be mine. She doesn't have a choice in the matter.

My heart pounded in my chest as I watched her launch into the air, twisting mid-jump before landing with the grace of a predator. She didn't smile, didn't revel in the moment.

I leaned against the railing, letting the cold metal bite into my palms as I watched her with hungry eyes. She didn't stop. She wouldn't stop. Not until she'd pushed herself past whatever limit she had set for herself tonight. But I could see it—the slight tremor in her legs, the way her breath came in ragged gasps, and all I could imagine was how much better it would be if she trembled under me and if I fucked her so good she couldn't breathe. I wanted that. I needed all the passion she put on the ice to be reflected in claw marks along my spine.

Pushing away from the railing, I stepped out from the shadows and onto the ice, my boots crunching softly against the cold surface. Josie didn't notice me at first, too caught up in her own personal battle. But as I approached, she faltered slightly, her eyes flicking up to meet mine.

For a moment, neither of us said anything. She stood there, chest heaving, eyes vast and wild, like a caged animal. I could see the sweat glistening on her brow, the flush in her cheeks. Her body screamed for rest, but her mind wouldn't let her quit.

"What move are you trying to do?" I said quietly, my voice low and even.

Out of breath, with her hands tightly propped on her hips, she narrowed her eyes on me. "And you are?"

"Answer the question." My voice was firm, eyes hooded.

"Answer mine."

"Christopher."

Her eyes widened, but she quickly schooled her features and bowed her head like the polite little princess she played all evening. "Christopher Jackson?"

"In the flesh," I smirked, my lips slipping to the side, crossing my arms over my chest. "Now, what move are you working on?"

"Mr. Jackson, I can assure you that I—" she stuttered, gliding closer to me, her hands dancing in front of her.

I cut off her rambling, narrowing my eyes on the pinks in her freckled cheeks. "You messed up a spin three minutes into your performance."

She paused, looking over her shoulder and lowering her voice as if we weren't alone. "You noticed?"

My gaze roamed over her body, taking in every inch. "I'm observant," I shrugged, wanting to mention how much I noticed about her, because a stumble was only the surface. But I restrained myself, knowing that patience is a virtue, even if mine was wearing thin.

She scoffed and bit her lip, her eyes flickering around the empty rink.

"We're alone, Josie. Tell me." My steps echoed throughout the stadium as I made my way closer to Josie. The scent of fresh snow and vanilla invaded my senses, and I had to swallow back the growl trying to escape my throat.

"It's a Biellmann spin. It's supposed to be simple." She shook her head, looking down at her bare legs, pink from the cold, and her hands shaking from frustration.

I pinched her chin, making her look me in the eye. Her breath caught in her throat. Her pink lips were slightly agape. Her green eyes, which looked like emeralds, glossed over and were wide as she stared at me.

"Explain it to me, princess," I whispered, my breath feathering over her face.

She took another breath, her words coming out slow, deliberate. "You start spinning, just like any other move. Then you reach back, grab your skate, and pull it up over your head... It's like—like you're trying to break yourself in half. Your leg is straight, but you have to keep spinning. Faster. Tighter."

Her voice faltered as I tilted her chin just a little higher, making her look at me, getting a peak of a perfect-like heart right behind her right ear.

"Your back arches so deep it feels like it might snap, but you have to hold it. You can't slow down. Everything has to stay perfectly balanced, or you fail." Her eyes flashed with frustration, like the memory of every failed attempt was burning through her.

"And where do you fail?"

She swallowed, her eyes darting from me, but I squeezed her chin tighter, pulling her damn near underneath me. Josie is so small I could toss her around with one hand, and her nerves radiate off her onto me in waves that I allow to satiate me until her fury returns.

"Fail?" Her nostrils flare. "I don't fail."

"Don't lie to me, little girl. You wouldn't be on this ice if you weren't failing." I licked my lips, my eyes trained on her face while hers darted to my lips. *Naughty girl*, turned on by the lips of a man fifteen years her senior.

"It's tighter." She whispered so low I barely heard her.

I watched the fire in her eyes flicker, the blush creeping up her neck as she tried to compose herself, but she was trembling—half with anger, half with something else. I tilted her chin higher, not letting her escape the moment.

"Tighter, huh?" I murmur, my voice low, teasing her, testing how far she'll let this go.

"Yes, tighter," she snapped, her breath coming faster. "The moment I pull my leg up, everything has to lock in—my core, back, even my hips. One tiny slip, one muscle out of place, and the spin goes wide. If I'm not tight, I lose control. I can feel it wobble."

I smirked, inching closer, my thumb brushing over the soft skin of her chin. "So that's where you're failing? You're not *tight* enough?" The words roll off my tongue slowly, like a challenge.

Her lips parted, the slightest hitch in her breath giving her away, but she kept her gaze locked on mine, refusing to back down. "I'm tight enough," she whispered, her voice sharp despite how she shivered beneath my touch.

I leaned in closer, my mouth just inches from hers, and I could feel the tension vibrating between us. "Prove it, then," I whisper against her lips. "Show me you can hold it together, princess."

In waves, heat danced off her body, and right when she was going to break and tell me to fuck off or show me how she takes command over her body, the man I was going kill for her came into the stadium.

"Why don't I hear your fucking skates?!" A man barked. I turned slowly, looked over my shoulder, and narrowed my eyes at the idiot. He was shorter than me and looked like a clean-cut, all-American skater.

"Because I'm talking to her," I growled, baring my teeth.

"Oh, Mr. Jackson, I am-"

"Who the fuck are you?" I snarled, making the more petite man in a fucking neon turtleneck flinch.

"I am Dylan. Josie's partner, right babe?"

Josie placed a small hand on the center of my back, sending flames rushing through me.

"Right." She whispered, moving around me.

"You let your partner talk to you like that?" I lowered my eyes to hers, ignoring the nervous twitching of the idiot.

"No. Dylan, I will practice when I want."

"Women, am I right, Jackson?! Don't know a hard day's work."

. . .

Heat surged through me, my jaw locking the moment that idiot's voice grated the air. I focused on Dylan, feeling the primal need to protect her spike in my chest. He had a smug grin plastered on his face, clearly trying to play buddy-buddy.

"You think that's funny?" I growled, my voice dangerously low as I stepped closer, towering over him. Dylan's smirk wavered.

"Come on man, you know what it takes to be at the top, and she's not putting the work in."

My eyes flicked to Josie—she was stiff, her expression unreadable, but I could see the tension in how she clenched her fists. She was annoyed, maybe even embarrassed by the idiot, but too polite to put him in his place.

"Not putting in the work?" I echoed, my voice low, dangerous.

Dylan chuckled, running a hand through his hair, but his laugh lacked real humor. "She's great, don't get me wrong. But you know how it is, man. Sometimes, they need a little...push. Otherwise, they fall behind."

Josie's lips parted, but no words came out. I saw her flinch just the tiniest bit, and that was all it took for me to lose the last thread of patience I had.

I stepped forward, closing the distance between Dylan and me, towering over him now. My voice was steady, lethal. "A push?" I said, narrowing my eyes. "That's what you call it?"

Dylan shifted, his cocky expression faltering for a second, but he still tried to keep up the act. "You don't get it, Jackson. She's stubborn. If I don't keep her in line, she'll never be ready for the big leagues. You've seen it yourself—she's slipping."

"Keep her in line?" I repeated slowly, letting the words hang in the air like a threat. My voice dropped, dark and cold. "What the fuck do you mean by that?"

"Stop it." Josie snapped, her body a paling pink and the phantom print of her hand against my spine ringing. "I need silence to practice."

"Josie-" I said, but she shook her head and kept her eyes down.

"Both of you need to leave, please; I need to practice." She spit out the words like venom before skating away to the other side of the stadium.

I took a step closer to Dylan, ready to give the obnoxious punk a warning, when the voice of the PR head of the Titans rang through the stadium. "Jackson! I have been looking all over for you. We need photos!"

A growl rolled through my chest, and Dylan flinched out of the way as I stalked out of the stadium. That would be the last time I would ever leave Josie unprotected.

Josie

.   .   .

Ten Months Later -- Present Day

Right foot slide. Left slide. Turn over your left shoulder. Scrape the right foot across the ice. Tuck and-

"Fuck!" I tumble on the ice again; the flurries of snow scraped up from the blades of my skates soak into my already wet pants. This is the twentieth time I have attempted to do a Mohawk Turn into a jump, a simple move I could have done in my sleep last season, and now, I can barely do anything more than a basic glide.

I rest my elbows on my knees, my right hand scratching at the loose curls from my bun around the nape of my neck. I almost forget I am not alone, but then the slow clapping from the sidelines erupts. My stomach free falls, and the sound of his skates gliding towards me grates across my skin.

"Better than last week." Dylan shrugs; his black thermal-lined pants come into my eye line, but I still don't want to look into his cocky green eyes. Dylan has a way of hurting me more than I can hurt myself, and that's saying something.

"Oh yeah, or are you just saying that?"

Dylan sighs, and I can tell his fingertips are gripping the bridge of his nose by the annoyed sound. "You asked me to be nicer."

"Nicer, not lie." I bark, my head jerks up, and I immediately regret it. Dylan used to be the most gorgeous man I had ever seen in my life. His green eyes have flecks of gold in them. His dark brown hair reminded me of the silkiness of milk chocolate, and his smile used to melt me to the core. Also, it's just not fair how he is lean and toned in all the right ways—that gets my panties wet—or used to, at least.

"Well, how about this, Golden Girl?" I cringe at the nickname from my youth, when everyone thought I was destined to be a gold medalist and my signature blonde, shoulder-length curly hair. "You're not even bronze level anymore."

My eyes widen, and my skin sets a blaze. I press my open palms into the biting ice of the rink, trying to cool down before I say anything I would regret, to the matching accessory of my career. "You wouldn't have hoped to be anywhere near the Olympic Circle if it wasn't for me."

Whoops, so much for not saying anything mean, but fuck him. I was the star. I was the one people came to see, and if it weren't for him and our old coach pushing me to do the death spiral, then I wouldn't be here. I fling my hand up at Dylan, and he locks his big hand around my freezing fingers, hissing at the sensation. A spark of satisfaction shoots through me at his twisted gaze, but I bite back the impending smile.

Dylan's eyes sharpen onto mine, and his grip tightens to the point I can feel my knuckles crack under his touch.

"Josie, I am the only reason anyone lets your stupid ass near the ice anymore; remember that."

"Oh, I'm sorry. I didn't know you had a lineup of women ready to be dropped onto the ice." I snarl, yanking my arm, but Dylan pulls me in closer against his chest.

His hand snakes around my waist, and from the outside looking in, we look like we're in love, doing the tango, and I am just so lost in his eyes. There was a time this was true, and we would be seconds from running into the locker room and warming each other up, but now I wouldn't let him touch me with a ten-foot pole or the five inches in his pants.

"Hockey tryouts are in ten. I need all skates off the ice." A gruff voice bellows from the stands.

Dylan doesn't look up. Instead, he sweeps his eyes to my lips and then back to my eyes as he speaks. "You got it, Coach Chris."

My nostrils twitch, and Dylan smirks at the slight rise he gets out of me before pushing me away, so I have to dig in my skates to stop. My bun loosens, and more strands fall in my face as I watch Dylan skate away and off the ice. My eyes flicker up to the scoreboard, the time beaming bright red at the top.

"Hockey tryouts are not for another two hours," I call up, looking at Coach Christopher Jackson, the best living player in NHL history and the new coach of the Northbrook Tigers, a team who made it to finals last year and bombed so hard the world had bet their ranking was a mistake. If Northbrook was going to play that badly, then no one should have let them in the darn arena; it was a disgrace. It was also the only thing that eclipsed the news of my head splitting and what everyone thinks is a career-ending injury.

Did I mention that Coach Jackson is also the only person in the world who can make my breath hitch and my body quake just by saying my name?

"He was in your face again." Coach says, leaning back in his bleacher seat right next to the left side of the arena. His long limbs stretch over three rows of benches as he watches me.

I turn to practice a trick I learned at six, a scratch spin. It's simple: start by grinding backward on an outside edge, then shift to a spinning position by pulling your free leg and arms inward to increase rotation speed while balancing on the ball of your skating foot. Easy, so when I have to hit the glass to brace myself from falling, I scream. "Shit!"

"Aye, watch your mouth, princess." Coach corrects, leaning forward in the stands.

He wears a gray thermal long-sleeve shirt, Timberland boots, and baby blue jeans. His thick black hair is smoothed back into a slick style, his beard is professionally trimmed, and he looks like the Greek sculptor Phidias sculpted every muscle on his body. If I didn't already know who he was, I'd think he was just a really hot senior and totally would give him my number.

"I'm not a princess," I growl, gliding along the rink's wall.

"You just threw a tantrum like a spoiled little girl, so *princess*." He quips; the sound of amusement rolls over his words, and it takes everything out of me not to growl again.

"I'm frustrated. I can't seem to..." Right in front of him, I pause with only the glass separating our gazes. He has the most amazing deep blue eyes I have ever seen. They look like a stormy ocean, and my core clinches at the thought of me caught in his fury or passion. I bet his opponents on the ice drop to their knees in mercy under his gaze.

"What?" His eyes narrow, and the storm eases through the eclipse of his black eyelashes. He sounds mad, but I can tell by the twitch in the corner of his lip that he is teasing me. "Get tight enough?"

"No, I'm not trying to do the Biellmann spin. I'm doing a scratch turn." I murmured. I haven't been able to be on the ice since the accident last winter, about three weeks after the Winter Showcase, where I first met Coach Jackson. The accident where Dylan dropped me and I crashed into the ice, my head cracked out, twelve stitches, a concussion. I was in my bed back in Minnesota with my mother for six months. She'd kill me if she knew I was back on the ice.

"You're scared of the ice,now?" He shrugs.

"I have never been scared of the ice."

"Okay." He nods, one of his plush pink lips poking out. "So go do your scratch turn."

I roll my eyes. "Oh fuck off."

"Excuse me?" The stern rasp in his voice heightens as he leans so close to the glass he is almost hanging off the seat.

"You just saw me fail, and you're demanding more of me?"

"If you're not afraid of the ice, do it again." He challenges.

I burn so hot my ears feel like they're on fire. Scoffing, I turn on my heels to skate to the other side of the rink.

"Don't skate away from me!" He growls, the creak of metal from the benches ringing through the arena.

"You're not my coach!" I bark back, my skates slicing against the ice, creating an off-beat rhythm from my huffing as I make a b-line to the lockers.

Who the hell does Coach Jackson think he is? I am not on his team of dumb hockey jocks knocking into each other on the ice. I am an Olympic-bound athlete. He's just a washed-up NHL player in fucking Maine, a coach for a D2 school, might I add, not even in the top twenty.

My anger burns away any bite of the cold from my falls. My skates clink against the concrete as I wind down to the locker rooms. My mind is still running wild.

"Coach is wrong, Josie," I whisper, my hands running over the raised scars along my forearms. "You were born to be on the ice. You aren't scared."

I yank at my laces, feeling the rough leather bite into my fingers as I wrestle with the skates. My hands are trembling, and my fingers are numb from the cold and fight. My muscles taunt with failure, another terrible practice where I feel further away from myself.

The skates won't come off fast enough, making it worse and forcing something resentful to boil inside me. I yank harder, finally wrenching one of them free, and I can't hold it in anymore. I hurl them across the room, the dull clatter of them hitting the lockers echoing in the space.

There is something satisfying about watching the skates clatter to the ground as if they mean nothing. I slam my other foot to the ground, yanking the second one free, and my breath comes in ragged, angry bursts.

My feet throb as they meet the cold air, raw and stinging, but it's nothing compared to the fire raging in my chest. The thick and suffocating silence presses down on me as if the whole room is mocking me, reminding me of everything that slipped away.

Alone in the cold, sterile locker room, the skates lay abandoned—useless—just like me. A slow clap echoes through the space, startling me. I spin around, my eyes landing on Coach Christopher Jackson, staring at me with a bored expression.

"You got it out of your system?"

I painfully pull my bottom lip into my mouth. My nostrils flare, and my knuckles curl into numbing a ball of anger. I step forward, eyes narrowed in on his glowing golden eyes. "Didn't I tell you to fuck off?"

He scoffs, rolling his neck on a deep breath. "I heard you; I just didn't think you would say it to my face."

"Why not?" I roll my eyes, placing both hands on my hips, a nasty smile on my face. "Because you're the big bad NHL veteran coach?"

"No, because I am fifteen years your senior."

"Is that supposed to mean something?"

"It means you should respect me." Coach Jackson growls.

. . .

The low rumble rolls over my skin like the bite of the ice. I take in a shaky breath, closing my eyes in a slow blink. My eyes lock on his, and the roll of his jaw makes my core clench.

"Respect is earned." I snarl. "You don't know anything about figure skating. You know nothing about me, saying that I am afraid of the ice...do you know how wild that is?"

"I know what I saw." He sighs, scrunching up the sleeves of his gray thermal shirt, showcasing a mirage of colorful ink encased in thick black lines.

There is nothing hotter than a man covered in tattoos with muscles that look like they could crush you into a million pieces. I yank my ponytail out of my head, suddenly feeling suffocated. I need to get out of these wet clothes and away from Coach Jackson's intense dark gaze. I need to breathe somewhere; I can't see my breath with every exhale. I need to be warm for the first time in my life. I need the sun but can't move; instead, I fist my wavy blonde stands and huff.

"You are afraid of the ice." Coach stretches his neck and arms, straining the veins in his forearms as he approaches me.

I shake my head, taking a step back with each of his steps forward because fuck this! He tackles people and runs after a puck all day. I am flinging my body into the air, hoping that asshole Dylan saves me from cracking my skull open again or that I extend my leg to the right more and catch myself before I fall.

"My life is on the line every time I skate," I whisper.

Coach Jackson stops just inches away, his eyes locked on mine. The air between us grows dense, and I can practically feel the heat radiating from him. I want to be closer, to run my hand along his skin and find where the core of his warmth is. I want his sun to be mine. I avoid his eyes, looking at my bare feet.

"You think hockey is just a game of chasing pucks? Whenever I stepped onto the ice every shift, someone could slam me into the boards hard enough to break bones. Or worse." His voice lowers to a ticklish whisper, crawling across my skin.

"That's different," I snap back, my voice rising in frustration. "You're wearing layers of padding, and you're in control. I'm out there in practically nothing, with blades strapped to my feet, hurling myself through the air—"

"Don't act like you've got it worse because you're spinning in sequins while we get bruises and bloodied."

My breath hitches, my mind racing, the frustration boiling over. "I'm not saying you don't get hurt, but—"

"But what? Our risks aren't valid because we wear helmets?" His jaw tightens, his stormy blue eyes blazing. "You want to talk about danger? I've seen guys go down and not get back up. I've been hit so hard I didn't know where I was. And guess what? I still get back on the ice."

His voice rings through the locker room, and my head tucks into my chest. I feel like I want to scream. I feel like I am in so much trouble that he has no excuse but to punish me. *Punish me? Have I lost my freaking mind?*

"You don't look like you want to be on that ice, " he whispers, his palm flat against the wall above me. His body encases me in a warm cocoon, and his smokey firewood scent invades my nostrils.

I freeze, watching the rise and fall of his chest, holding my breath like it is the only thing that will keep me alive. The ice is my home. The ice is everything to me. I can't be afraid of the one thing that makes me, right?

"Let's say you're right, Coach." I look up at him through my eyelashes, slowly licking my dry lips and watching as his eyes follow the lines of my tongue. "What do I do now?"

"You let me coach you."

I lean back against the wall and click it to the right. "And what makes you qualified?"

His eyes darken, and I gulp, fidgeting when he spreads his lips into a Cheshire smile. "I can make you fear me more than the ice."

Chapter 3

Christopher

"Again." I bark.

The clatter of groans and skates rings through the stadium. The boys on my team aren't special, but they aren't bad. They just need discipline, something only one of my star students has: Josie. She sits on the other side of the stadium despite my politely asking her to sit next to me, which only proves to me that next time, I won't ask.

Asking with her has gotten me nowhere; she avoided me for three weeks after agreeing to let me coach her. It's now damn near fucking Thanksgiving, and I haven't seen her once. I had to pick her up from her final class today at 4 p.m. to make her come to the rink. I told her if she moved, she would be suspended from the rink because she needed my permission to use it anyway.

Having Josie at tryouts isn't ideal. The boys kept whistling at her and earned a round of suicides because they got whipped up into a frenzy when she put her hair into a ponytail. I mean, who could blame them? This girl is mine, and I am not much of a sharer. She doesn't know that yet, so I can't blame her for her flirtations, but I can punish everyone around her for looking.

Right now, the boys are on their final lap, and I am more than ready to kick them out of the stadium, peel off that princess layer, and give all my attention to my little hellion. She is doing the terribly naughty task of chewing on the end of her pen as she marks up an old copy of *The Tempest*. How fitting that my temptation only learns more ways to torment me.

"Kelsey, you're behind!" My assistant coach and best friend since grade school, Caleb, barks at the players. Caleb and I have been inseparable since birth and probably will be that way until death. Caleb has dirty blonde hair with dyed green tips, no tattoos because the punk is scared of needles, but a bright smile that practically melts panties.

He elbows me in the side, lowering his voice. "You're staring."

"Can't help it." I automatically said back, watching as she pulled at her leg warmers and shuffled her legs to get comfortable on the bleachers.

Caleb scoffed, shaking his dirty blonde hair in his face. "The boys are skating over; tear your eyes away from the jail bait before they notice."

I dart my eyes back to the ice, muttering in a low tone. "She is perfectly legal."

"Oh, I know, but is it perfectly moral?"

"Shut up." I scoff, letting out a low chuckle before averting my attention back to the players lining up in front of me.

"Well, boys, you aren't complete disappointments." Caleb laughs, but I narrow my eyes on the players, school my face to look uninterested and grab the clipboard I've been writing notes on all practice off the bench.

"Isaiah, your left is always open!" I bark, watching the kid straighten up, his face flushing with frustration. "Every damn time, you're leaving a gap wide enough to drive a truck through. Fix it, or next time you're benched."

Conner shifts nervously next to him, already sensing he's next. "And you, Conner," I say, not bothering to lower my voice. "How many times do I have to tell you? You're hesitating on the puck. Hockey is not the time for second-guessing. You see an opening, you take it. Not tomorrow. Not when you're ready. Right now."

He nods stiffly, but I can see the doubt in his eyes. I roll mine, turning to the next player. "Hunter, stop skating like a damn ballerina. This isn't a dance class; keep your stance low. You're going to get wrecked if you keep gliding around like that."

Hunter opens his mouth, probably ready with some excuse, but I cut him off with a sharp wave of my hand. "I don't want to hear it. If you don't start skating like you have a spine, you'll be sitting in the stands next time."

I ignore him, moving on to the next. "Mason, your stick handling is sloppy as hell. It's embarrassing. If you can't keep the puck under control, what the hell are you even doing out here?"

I catch movement in the corner of my eye—Josie's still sitting on the bleachers, adjusting her leg warmers, a faint smirk on her lips. My chest tightens for a second, and I grit my teeth, forcing myself to focus back on the team.

"Thomas," I growl, "You're dragging ass. If I see you skating that slow in a game, you're off the ice. Period."

Thomas's eyes widen, and I see the panic settling in. Good. Fear works.

"And Kelsey," I add, turning toward the forward who's been barely keeping up with drills. "You're behind. Again. Pick up the pace, or I'm sending you to run laps until you puke."

I roll my shoulders back and fold my arms over my chest, signaling to Caleb that I am done.

Caleb claps his hands, stepping forward. "Alright, that's enough for today. Hit the showers, all of you."

As the boys shuffle out, I lower my voice so only Caleb can hear. "Keep them out of the rink."

"Got it, boss. Make sure she's not too loud. I can't really make the boys cover their ears." Caleb jokes, and I push him so hard out of the penalty box he almost falls on his face.

"Josie!" Mason, a brown-haired, hulk-looking boy, smiles, waving at her as he makes his way from the locker room and closer to her. A wide grin splits his face, and I feel my heart drop as she looks up at him, her smile brightening like a damn sunrise.

She shifts her book off her lap, focusing entirely on him.

"Hey, I was wondering—"

"Mason!" I bark, my voice reverberating off the walls, a visceral snarl slipping through clenched teeth.

"Coach, come on!" He pouts, gesturing toward Josie as if she were a prize to be won, his expression a mix of annoyance and disbelief.

"Now!" I snap, gripping the clipboard in my hand so tight I feel like it is going to snap. My heart races, the primal urge to stake my claim overwhelming. "Or you'll be doing suicides until you vomit."

Mason's eyes flashed with irritation, but my glare hardened his resolve. He opens his mouth to protest but catches my deadly stare, the muscles in his jaw tightening. After a moment of hesitation, he exhales sharply, turning on his heel. His massive frame stomping away, the ice echoing under his heavy boots as if the rink itself were protesting his retreat.

As he disappears around the corner, I feel the tension in my shoulders ease slightly, but my focus remains fixed on Josie, who is staring at me with a knowing grin on her face.

"You're a real charmer, do you know that?"

I ignore her question, calmly crossing the ice in my boots. "Why aren't you in your skates?"

"I'm sorry, I didn't have time. Someone dragged me out of Econ."

"You have a pair in your locker." I narrow my eyes on her, crossing my arms over my chest.

"Am I allowed to go to my locker to get my skates, oh, benevolent one?" She rolls her eyes, matching my body language as she crosses her arms over her chest.

"Stop with the back talk Josie, before you piss me off."

She scoffs, skipping down the stadium steps with a tempting look of challenge on her face. "Or what?"

My feet come to an abrupt halt, just inches from the glass barrier that separates us.

She stands three steps above me, the dim light casting a soft glow on her face. Her eyes narrow, piercing through the air between us, a mix of challenge and intrigue. A wicked grin spreads across my lips, the heat of my desire igniting a possessive fire within me.

I lean closer, my heart pounding in my chest, feeling the electricity crackle in the air. With a twisted smile, I revel in the intoxicating thrill of the chase. She will soon realize that she belongs to me. There's no turning back now; I need to test the waters to see how far I can push her.

"Or my handprint will be permanently printed on your ass," I growl, my voice laced with a dangerous edge.

She pales, and for a second, I think she is going to run. I can practically see the thoughts racing through her mind as she considers running from me. But I won't let that happen. I can already feel my grip tightening on her, dragging her back to me, kicking and fucking screaming.

What the hell am I going to do with an unwilling obsession? She has to be mine. I mean, there is no way around it—she is either mine or no one's. But just as I am about to run to the opening and grab her, her cheeks flush in that sexy, rosy pink, and she slides the corner of her bottom lip into her mouth.

"Excuse me?" She gasps, placing both hands on her hips and cocking her head to the side.

"You heard me, Josie. Pick one: get your skates or get my hand across that tight little ass of yours." My voice is deadly calm, a stark contrast to the steady increase of my heart banging against my chest. I walk closer to the opening of the rink and into the stands.

Josie doesn't move, but her eyes are trained on my body as I place both hands on the rink's opening, gripping the walls so tight my knuckles burn, but it's the only thing I can do not to touch her.

"You're not supposed to talk to your students like this."

"You're not officially my student," I grunt, my head hanging between my shoulders as I look up at her with hooded eyes. "Remember?"

She shifts her weight on her feet, that fucking lip sliding between her teeth again. My blood boils at the sight of her teeth nibbling at her full pink bottom lip, a habit she probably doesn't even realize she has. Shaking my head to clear it, I force myself to focus.

"Stop that."

"Stop what?" She rolls her eyes and adds that to the list of things I need to punish her for.

"Biting your fucking lip."

"Or what?" She narrows her eyes, purposely biting her lips harder.

"Or I will bite it for you," I growl, snapping my head.

She meets my gaze with a defiant glint in her eyes, a small smile playing on her lips as she descends the steps towards me. "Then you better make it hurt," she says.

I suck in a shuddering breath, desperate to calm the storm raging in my chest. This girl is everything I've ever wanted, and she's right in front of me, tauntingly perfect. Right now, she could break me or make me whole, and I'm powerless to stop her.

"Is that what you want?" I hiss, my voice barely above a whisper. "You want me to make it hurt?"

She takes another step forward, her eyes never leaving mine as she shudders. She bites her lip again, a small gesture that makes my heart pound in my chest.

"Yes," she says softly, her voice barely audible over the sound of my own heartbeat.

"Go get your skates on," I growl.

"Boo," she pouts, standing right on the other side of the barrier, her eyes sparkling with want. "Such a tease."

I can see the hunger in her eyes as she stands just inches away from me, separated by a thin barrier.

Temptation courses through my veins, and I slam my fist against the glass, causing her to jump back. Her eyes are wide in fear, but the rise and fall of her chest reveals an underlying desire. The flush on her cheeks betray her arousal, showing that she wants me just as much as she may fear me, or maybe she wants that too, to push me until I make her quiver in fear, in want, in need.

"I won't be teasing for much longer. Move it, Richards," I snarl, my patience wearing thin.

"Yes, coach." She nods, turning on her heels towards the lockers.

I hold my breath until I can no longer hear the click of her heels fade into the distance. My pulse thunders in my ears, but it's not from exertion—it's from her. Fucking hell, what is this girl doing to me? She's all I think about. All I see. I'm chasing her around campus like some lovesick idiot, screaming at her in the rink like a madman, watching her every damn move during practice like she's the only thing on this ice that matters.

And maybe she is.

I try to shake the thought, but it lingers, gnawing at me. I've never been consumed like this, not by hockey, fame, or anything. It's her. Always her. Josie *fucking* Richards. I grind my teeth, pacing the empty rink like a caged animal. She's beneath my skin, lodged in my veins. It's more than desire now —a sickness, a craving. Something I can't control, and I hate it. I fucking hate it.

I move deeper onto the rink, trying to put as much space between us as humanly possible, but it doesn't feel like enough. She isn't even within ten feet of me, and I smell her all around me - vanilla and fresh snow.

I stare at the ice as I rub at the fresh tattoo on my chest. It's only been a few weeks, but I can feel her stitched into my skin even deeper than her name already is.

Her routines play on repeat in my head. Every spin, every jump, every damn smile she throws at those idiots who think they have a shot with her. I can't stand the thought of anyone else looking at her like I do. Touching her. They don't get to— they haven't earned that right.

Only I get to look at her like that. Only I—

My spiraling thoughts screech to a halt when I hear the soft shuffle of footsteps. My body tenses, and I inhale sharply, my heart thudding in my chest.

The familiar sound of her skates hitting the ice fills the rink. She's wearing them. The faint slide of blades on cold, smooth ice sends a chill through me, grounding me in the moment.

I don't turn around, don't let her see how twisted up I am inside, how I've been unraveling since the second she walked out of here. I let the silence hang between us, heavy, suffocating, until her voice—small, hesitant, but with that edge of defiance—breaks through the tension.

"Where do you want me?"

On my face. Is the first thing I think but I choke it down.

I turn slowly, my gaze as cold as the ice beneath us.

"On the ice," I say, my voice icy and distant, betraying none of the chaos inside me.

Continue reading Pucking Christmas Triplets Surprise is now Available FREE With Kindle Unlimited and Paperback

ABOUT THE AUTHOR

Self acclaimed Certified Reverse Harem Vixen | Sophie J. Rivers crafts steamy tales where passion meets puck! Think locker room antics, heart-thumping love triangles, and heat that melts the ice. Dive into stories that'll leave you breathless and craving for more. #PuckBunniesAndPolyamory

Follow Sophie J Rivers on Facebook to be the first to know when her next book becomes available.

Manufactured by Amazon.ca
Acheson, AB

16120886R00046